This Little Tiger book belongs to:

_____

_____

_____

_____

For Margaret, with love – M C B

For my Mum and Dad – G S

LITTLE TIGER PRESS
An imprint of Magi Publications
1 The Coda Centre, 189 Munster Road, London SW6 6AW
www.littletigerpress.com

First published in Great Britain 2011
This edition published 2011

Text copyright © M Christina Butler 2011
Illustrations copyright © Gavin Scott 2011
M Christina Butler and Gavin Scott have asserted their rights
to be identified as the author and illustrator of this work under
the Copyright, Designs and Patents Act, 1988

A CIP catalogue record for this book is available
from the British Library

Printed in China

2 4 6 8 10 9 7 5 3

Hot Cross Bunny!

M Christina Butler

Gavin Scott

LITTLE TIGER PRESS
London

It was a bright, crisp morning.
"Wheee!" squeaked Little Daisy
Rabbit, doing big bunny hops
through the woods.

"Look at the buds on the
trees!" cried Mummy Rabbit.
"And the new shoots growing,"
said Daddy Rabbit.

Mummy Rabbit was very excited when they got home. "Spring is just around the corner!" she sang.

"What is spring?" asked Daisy, frowning.

"Birds singing, flowers everywhere," replied Mummy Rabbit dreamily.

"Playing in the stream!" cried Archie and Sam.

"We won't be needing these!" smiled Mummy Rabbit, hanging up her woolly hat and scarf. "Can I have your hat please, Daisy?"

"*Oh no*, Mummy!" said Daisy. "Granny made it for me, and it's my *very favourite*!"

"You can't wear a woolly hat in spring!" laughed Sam.

"Wear it as long as you like, Daisy," said Mummy Rabbit gently. "But you might get tired of it."

"NEVER!" replied Daisy, shaking her head.

"I shall NEVER take my hat off," Daisy muttered as she ate her supper.

"I shall wear my hat forever," she gurgled in the bath.

"Forever... and ever... and ever!"

she murmured as she snuggled up and drifted off to sleep.

The next day Daisy was playing ball in the garden when she saw three primroses under the hedge.

"*Oh no!*" she gasped. "What are you doing here? We don't want spring in our garden!"

And she picked
the primroses and
popped them in
the dustbin!

Later in the week, Daisy
went to fly her kite.
Suddenly, a chirpy
sparrow began to sing.

Some blackbirds and a thrush
joined in.
"Get away, you birds,"
cried Daisy, waving her arms
in the air. "*Shoo! Shoo!* and take
spring with you!"

But a few days later, the garden was **filled** with birds and flowers. Spring was **everywhere!**

"Isn't spring wonderful?" smiled Mummy Rabbit.

"**NO!**" shouted Daisy, as cross as could be. "I don't want spring! I'm wearing my hat forever!"

Then one very sunny day, Granny called by.
"Anyone at home?" she asked cheerily.
"I thought we might have a picnic."
"Yippee! Granny's here!" cried Daisy.

"Why don't you take your hat off, Daisy?"
said Mummy Rabbit before they set off.
"You'll be too hot."

"No thank you," Daisy replied,
chasing after her brothers.

"Race you to the stream!" squeaked Daisy,
running through the wood.

She jumped in . . . *splosh!*

Archie and Sam followed . . . *sploosh!*

Splish! splash! they paddled up
and down.

Daddy Rabbit found a sunny
spot for the picnic and after
a while, everyone sat down.

But as Daisy nibbled her
dandelion salad,
her woolly hat began
to itch.

And by the time she had
her strawberry jelly, she
was feeling **very** hot
and rather fed up!

"What a hot cross bunny you look!"
said Granny. "Take your hat off, dear."
"I can't! You made it for me, Granny,
and it's **my very favourite!**"
sobbed Daisy.

"Oh, Daisy," Granny smiled, giving her
a big hug. "We'll keep your hat safe
until the cold weather comes again."
Then she whispered, "I've just
had a good idea."

"We're going for a walk," Granny said
in a loud voice. "We won't be long."
And off they went into the wood.

When they came back, Daisy was wearing
a hat made of feathers!

"It's my *spring* hat!" she cried.

"Brilliant!" chuckled Archie and Sam.

"Clever Granny!" smiled Mummy.

And Daisy laughed as she skipped and
twirled in her new *very favourite* hat!

Take your hat off to your favourite Little Tiger books . . .

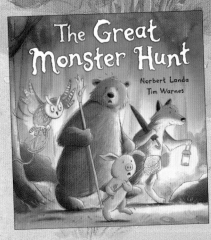